The Cat Who Wore a Pot on Her Head

(Original title: Bendemolena)

by Jan Slepian and Ann Seidler
illustrated by Richard E. Martin

SCHOLASTIC BOOK SERVICES

NEW YORK • TORONTO • LONDON • AUCKLAND • SYDNEY • TOKYO

ISBN 0-590-31595-1

12 11 10 9 8 7 6 5 4 3 2 1

Printed in the U.S.A.

0 1 2 3 4 5/8
18

There once was a cat named Bendemolena. She lived in a house on Cat Street, where cats and kittens lived all together. Brothers and sisters, cousins and friends were in and out and all about. What a noisy place it was!

One day when Bendemolena was playing, she found a shiny pot. She put it on her head. Suddenly all the noise was gone. She liked the quiet so much, she decided to wear the pot over her ears all the time.

The same day, Mother Cat said to Bendemolena and her nine little brothers and sisters, "I have to take care of a sick friend this afternoon. But, oh, dear! How am I going to clean the house and cook your supper, too?"

"Don't worry," said her kittens. "When you come home, supper will be ready and the house all clean. We'll take care of everything."

Mrs. Cat took Bendemolena with her to the sick friend's house. "I brought her to run errands," Mrs. Cat told her sick friend.

And soon Mrs. Cat wanted something. "Bendemolena, Bendemolena, run home and tell your brothers and sisters that it's time to put the fish on to bake."

Bendemolena didn't hear what her mother had said. Her ears were still under the pot. Everything she heard was all mixed up.

"Did she say to put the smish on to fake or to put the bish in the lake?" Bendemolena wondered as she ran home. "Oh! She must have said to put soap in the cake!

"Mama wants you to put soap in the cake," she told her brothers and sisters. All the kittens wanted to please Mother, so they put soap in the cake.

Almost as soon as Bendemolena got back to her mother, Mrs. Cat said, "Bendemolena, Bendemolena, I forgot to tell the children to put the soup on to heat. Run home and tell them to put the soup on to heat."

Again Bendemolena didn't hear very well because of the pot. "Put the boop on the beep? Mup the moop on the feep? . . . Oh! She must have said to iron the meat!"

"Mama says to iron the meat," she told the kittens at home. They all wanted to please Mother, so they got out the iron and ironing board, and ironed the meat.

All afternoon Bendemolena ran back and forth, telling her brothers and sisters what Mother wanted them to do.

Once Mrs. Cat said, "Bendemolena, Bendemolena, run home and tell the children to sweep out the hall."

"Feep out the ball? Meep out the mall? Gleep biddy ball? . . . Oh! Mother must have said to hang the chairs on the wall," Bendemolena decided.

"Mama wants you to hang the chairs on the wall," Bendemolena told the other kittens. The children all wanted to please Mother, so they got out the hammer and nails and hung the chairs up just like pictures.

Soon all the neighbors gathered around the house to watch. There were so many watching that Bendemolena had to crawl between their legs to get back to her mother.

Once again Bendemolena's mother had a message for the children. "Tell them to be sure to leave the key in the lock. Remember, leave the key in the lock."

Bendemolena raced home, saying to herself, "Gleeve the bee in the smock? Smick the smee on the sock? Sickee wee wubby gock? . . . Oh! She must have said to sew clothes on the clock."

"Sew clothes on the clock," Bendemolena told her brothers and sisters. And to please their mother, that is what they did.

Bendemolena again ran back to her mother.

"Bendemolena, Bendemolena, supper must be nearly ready. Go tell the children to make something to drink," Mother said.

"Make wiffily sink? Wump buffalo bink? . . . Oh! She must have said to put a horse in the sink!"

21

When Bendemolena told her brothers and sisters what Mother had said, they asked Mr. Horse, who lived down the street, if he would stand in the sink just to please their mother.

By this time, animals had come from all over to see for themselves what was happening at Mrs. Cat's house. There were big animals and small animals and in-between size animals.

Mrs. Cat was almost ready to leave her sick friend when she said, "Bendemolena, Bendemolena, run home and ask one of your brothers to fix my chair."

"Up in the air, sticky pear, purple hair? . . ." By the time Bendemolena got home, she decided her mother had said "Ask in a bear." And to please Mother, the kittens asked in a big, friendly bear from the crowd.

Just then Mrs. Cat came home.
She saw soap bubbles rising out of the cake,
And meat on the ironing board ready to bake.

She saw chairs on the wall,
And a bear in the hall.

She saw the clock dressed in pink,
And a horse in the sink.

And then under her chin, ten kittens marched in.

"What is the meaning of this?" Mrs. Cat cried.

"Surprise! Surprise!" said the kittens. They thought they had pleased their mother. They thought they had done just what she wanted. "We all did our best!" they called out.

But Bendemolena was still mixed up. "Ask in the rest?" she said to herself. Bendemolena threw open the door and called, "Everyone come in!"

27

Mrs. Cat looked at all the neighbors and friends. She looked at Bendemolena's head. Then she looked at her smiling kittens. She just couldn't stay angry. She knew it was all the fault of the pot.

"Everyone can stay for supper," said Mother Cat.

But she took the pot off Bendemolena's head and made two holes for ears in it. Then she put it back on Bendemolena.

"Bendemolena, Bendemolena, give me a hug," said Mrs. Cat. And did Bendemolena give her mother a bug or a rug? No! She gave her mother just what she wanted.